Miss E.W. Simonson

Jan

A tale of the early history of Brooklyn

Miss E.W. Simonson

Jan   .
A tale of the early history of Brooklyn

ISBN/EAN: 9783337088583

Printed in Europe, USA, Canada, Australia, Japan

Cover: Foto ©Andreas Hilbeck / pixelio.de

More available books at **www.hansebooks.com**

J A N:

A TALE OF

THE EARLY HISTORY OF BROOKLYN.

BY

A. L. O. B.

BROOKLYN, N. Y.

ORPHANS' PRESS—CHURCH CHARITY FOUNDATION.

1883.

PREFACE.

HIS story was written for the children of Brooklyn, that they may remember, when they read the history of colonial days, that our forefathers suffered the same hardships as other settlers, and emptied as much tea in New York harbor as the Bostonians did there.

JAN.

I.

ONE pleasant day in May, 1623, a vessel was sailing up a bay. After passing through a narrow strait, and around an island, it was heading for the land before it.

It was a strange looking vessel, with round bow and stern, different from the pointed ones we are familiar with. On the deck were assembled all the passengers, in groups of two and three, or families, with their chests and beds. Weak and wan were many of them, for they had been two long months on their voyage, sailing across the ocean.

Fierce storms had driven them back, until they were almost discouraged ; but at last, the morning before, they had opened their eyes and looked upon the green land and the hills which appeared so strange to them, accustomed to the flat level land of Holland. They would hardly retire to their berths the night before, for fear the land might prove an island, and disappear before morning ; but no, in the morning it was still there, and Captain May assured them if they continued to have favorable winds, they would soon reach New Amsterdam, their destination.

At the forward end of the boat sat a woman, still ill and weak; by her side stood a boy, a short, round, red-cheeked Holland boy, the first Jan Van Scoy, who had not had one day's illness since they left home. He had learned to climb the masts and tell the ropes as well as the oldest sailor. He had enjoyed every day of the voyage, but was as happy as the rest to know they would soon be on land again.

His mother had been so ill on the voyage, he had been afraid she would die, and be wrapt in a piece of sail-cloth, and buried in the sea, as several of their friends who had started with them had been ; but on this their last day on the water, she had revived, and walked up the cabin stairs.

The vessel sailed so close to the shore they could hear the singing of the birds, and see the blossoms on the trees. The water was smooth and glittered in the sunlight ; the sky was blue and clear, and every eye was bright and every heart glad, for they expected so much happiness in this wonderful land. They could see on the point of a long narrow neck of land, between two rivers, a house low and square, built of logs, the only one in all that wilderness, built for the traders

of the West India Company, who bought
furs from the Indians who inhabited the rest
of Manhattan Island. The traders called
this settlement of one house " New Amsterdam," after old Amsterdam, their home in the
Fatherland.

Jan, who had very keen eyes, shouted that
he could see men walking around the house.
Presently he said he could see several men
running down to the shore, and then, as the
distance lessened between the boat and shore,
the rest recognized their friends. They
shouted and waved to each other. Women
with tears rolling down their cheeks stretched
out their hands to those on the shore. Oh,
joy to see their loved ones, whom the children had almost forgotten !

Before the small boats reached the shore,
the men walked into the water to meet them,
and catching up the children, carried them to
the shore and into the "Trading House."

Soon the re-united families were gathered together, talking over the years since they had met. Jan, with the rest of the boys, formed themselves into an exploring party, and was up on the top of the house before the rest were entirely in it. They next visited the storehouse, and viewed the skins of animals they had never seen ; then stretched their limbs by playing tag around the immense trees, until the gates were locked for the night and they were obliged to go in.

Thirty families came over in the " New Netherlands," most of whom started the next day with Captain May, who decided to sail up the river Hendrick Hudson had discovered, as far as the next trading fort.

For some weeks Jan and his mother remained at the house at New Amsterdam, when his father, placing them and the household goods they had brought from Holland in a boat, rowed across the Ooest River to

Sewanacky, the Island of Shells, as the natives called the present Long Island. He had bought of Penhawitz, chief of the Canarsee tribe, a tract of land on the shore opposite the trading house, for a scarlet blanket. Here he had raised an Indian cabin of skins drawn over four poles, driven in the ground at equal distances. The ground was carpeted with pine needles. A pile of furs in one corner could be spread over the floor for beds at night. When the table was placed against the side of the tent, with the pewter meat dish and spoons shining upon it, the hour glass on the swinging shelf; the tulip, brought so many miles across the sea, planted beside the door, it was quite a home.

The next day friendly Indians came to see them. Jan looked at the strange people with the same curiosity with which they regarded him. The men dressed in skins, their dark faces painted red, green and yellow, the tall feathers waving in their hair, gravely smoking their pipes. The guttural talk of the women as they looked him over and over, and admired the bright buttons on his jacket, made him tremble for fear they might take it off him, for it was his best one. The others were not unpacked.

When the darkness deepened and they were alone, he could not sleep for the howling of the wolves in the forest around the cabin.

The next morning he accompanied his father down to the shore, and saw him depart in his row-boat; then hastened back to his mother, who could ill disguise her fear of the red men, as they looked upon her with their piercing black eyes when they passed the door. Her husband had explained to her that under no consideration must she close her door upon her Indian friends, for they would resent it. He had learned by experience that they would treat you as you treated them.

She sat in the door-way on a high back leather-covered chair she had brought over with her, and watched Jan cook the Indian corn on a fire built upon a pile of stones, and saw the braves in their canoes going and coming from the trading house with their furs; they were mostly of the Canarsee tribe, who lived a few miles across the island.

Amid their loneliness, Jan and his mother talked of the goodly land they had found, not recalling, as the waves rippled to their feet, the land their fellows were laving, but onward to the time when others would share with them those hills crowned with flowering dog-wood and horse-chestnuts, and the valleys smiling with trailing arbutus and the blue violet which filled the air with fragrance.

When Jan's father returned home that

night, he brought strings of wampum, or Indian money ; round, flat pieces of shell, pol-
ished smooth, which the Canarsie tribe were
famed for making. When through the summer there came to their door squaws selling
their wares. Jan would pay them in their own
coin. These Indian women would walk miles
to sell turkeys or fish to the white men.

The braves spent their time in making arrow-heads of quartz, of different shapes, some
pointed, some leaf shape, but all regular and
even. Occasionally they varied their lives
by a battle with another tribe, perhaps the
Manhattoes, who were their bitter enemies ;
they also made their own copper tobacco
pipes, but the women raised the tobacco they
smoked, and were the beasts of burden.

There came to their door one day a young
squaw, whose face was painted black. They
knew the woman and had often traded with
her, but they never saw her look so be-

fore. She said nothing as she stepped in, and quietly laid her baby down on the furs by Mrs. Van Scoy, and sat down on the floor beside them. Jan hastened to place food before her, but she said "Aneki's heart is full of tears; she cannot eat, for her Brave has gone to the Happy Hunting Grounds;" and then, amid her tears, she proceeded to tell that in battle an arrow-head had entered his arm, and caused his death not many days afterwards.

They buried him sitting, with his bow and arrow and wampum beside him, with venison and fruits to make him strong in the battles he had gone to; and she would mourn for him until the paint had worn off her face by her tears.

That autumn was the most beautiful Jan's mother had ever known. She was too ill to walk far, but could lie on her bed of skins and look through the open doorway on the

heights aglow with sumac bushes and the yellow of the maples, shaded with the deep green
of the pines. After a few cool days came
the warm Indian summer, when she could
lean on Jan's arm and walk slowly down to
the beach. But the beauty departed from hill
and valley ; the fallen leaves choked the path
to the spring; the leafless branches of the
trees moaned around the cabin ; the cold air
penetrated the skins of the tent, and the days
grew very long to Mrs. Van Scoy. She
longed for the narrow streets, and the brick
houses of old Amsterdam ; the Sundays
when, upon the ringing of church bells, the
Burgher and his family walked in line to
church. She talked to Jan of the old scenes,
and dreamt of them at night.

The kind women brought in corn and
baked it, but it grew distasteful to her, and
there were no more provisions in the cabin.
The snow began to cover the dead vines which

swayed against the one window. All the
meadow was clothed in white; the ice formed
over the river, and it was becoming dangerous for Jan to try to get to the trading
house for food, for now his father had become ill with lung fever.

Every day his mother's cough became
worse, and she lay looking out upon the bay,
watching; always watching for the first bird
of spring, for then they expected a vessel
from Holland—which sight never gladdened
her eyes. For while the last snow covered the
ground, she went home, where she would be
no more hungry, and where there would be
no more sea.

The chief sent six of his braves to carry the
coffin; the traders came from New Amsterdam, and followed with the one mourner.
After them walked the whole tribe, in single
file, down the path through the woods, to the
edge near the shore: There they laid her to

rest, where the rays of the setting sun would rest upon her grave. In a few days they performed the same office for Jan's father, and then Jan was alone in the world.

His friends gathered together his few valuables and took them with Jan over to the trading house, and the cabin was left alone, until Jan should be old enough to occupy it. In the mean while the tobacco his father had planted was to be sold and laid away for him.

2

II.

THE years passed away. Jan was a strong, stout boy of sixteen years. He still lived at the fort, which had replaced the old trading house. A meeting was held every Sunday in the top floor of a horse mill, while a church was being built for Dominie Bogardus. Several boweries or farms were laid out on Manhattan Island. Jan saw the first shipload of slaves land at New Amsterdam, and his heart ached for them, as they lie cramped and chained in the stone house.

The Canarsie tribe appeared to adopt Jan. He roamed the woods with the Indian boys, who taught him to hunt the bear and deer, and lie under the trees and sleep through the warm days, or set around the camp fire in the winter and listen to their stories and legends.

A mile back from the river on the Gowanus Creek, was their great maize fields, where the women raised all the maize for the tribe. Jan often spent whole days there, helping the women and boys, or playing with the little red skins lying on the grass. At their great feast, when the corn was ripe, the chief sent him a piece of bark, marked with curious characters, and signed with his name, —a bow and arrow—which was intended for an invitation for him to join their sports. Jan returned, with his acceptance to the chief, a bright pewter tobacco box. When he reached the camp, the women were sitting in their tent doors with the girls and small boys; the braves were all seated in a circle around a man they called their priest, who, taking a piece of money from each, placed it all upon the top of the tents. Then he brought in a beast he called the " Evil Spirit." While the attention of the tribe, paralyzed with wonder and fear, is fixed upon this evil one, the priest collects the money from the tent tops, and appropriates it to himself. Then calling in a "Good Spirit," to drive out the evil one, the dance commences.

Each man holding a small stick in his hand, with which he strikes the ground, shouts and jumps ; then whirls around and around in a mad dance, the women gradually joining in. The men jump in the fire in their frenzy, and seizing fire-brands, throw them in the air. Jan shook with terror at the sight of their madness, and stealing softly behind their tents, away from the light of their camp fire, he crept along until the woods hid him. Then as the twilight was coming on, he ran along the narrow path, as it was not safe to be out in the woods after dark on account of the wolves. Slipping and falling, he ran on, until he saw his own bright fire burning before his tent to keep off the wolves. Sinking into a high-backed chair, he covered his face with his hands to keep out those fearful faces, but he could not sleep that night, and at daybreak rowed over to the fort, and for many weeks he would hear in his dreams those frightful yells, which never appeared to him to come from human throats. It cost him some effort to go back again to their camp, but in time the bad impression wore off.

Some of the Walloons, who had settled at Albany, came down to New Amsterdam, and bought land from the Canarsie tribe on Sewanhacky, or Longe Island, as the Dutch called it. across the Ooest River. Adrianse Bennet bought the next place to Jan's. Jacques Bentryn settled at Gowanus. Back from the river a mile or so, a few more settlers built stone houses, and called it Breuck-

len. Back still further, was a settlement called Flatbush, which was the market town,
where Jan, after he took possession of his
own land, brought his tobacco to sell, which
his honest Dutch neighbors said was the finest
in the market.

One day Jan was coming down the Bowery
when he saw a white man give an Indian
liquor, and then steal his skins. Jan watched
beside him until he awoke, when he felt his
loss and vowed vengeance. Jan gave him
money, and he departed, and the next Jan
heard was that he had killed two white men,
and then fled to his own nation. When the
sachems heard of this they offered strings of
wampum to Governor Kieft as restitution,
but this the Governor refused. At the same
time the different tribes were at war among
themselves, but they still believed in and
trusted the white man, and came in
droves to New Amsterdam for protection.

Some crossed over to the Jersey shore, that they might still be near the White Father.

There was a feast at one of the boweries, and Jan had been all the afternoon trying his strength jumping and racing with the other youths, and now was walking back to the fort, stiff and tired, when he saw Governor Kieft's soldiers drawn up before the fort. What in the world could it mean? He hurried along, and at last broke into a run as he neared them, and met Cornelius De Vreis, a landholder from Staten Island, who was going with equal rapidity to the fort.

He asked him the cause of this sudden order of march, but could get no answer, as De Vreis began to talk to the Governor; then he found they were going over to the Jersey shore to murder the Indians who had placed themselves under their protection. De Vreis begged the Governor to countermand the order, but he was obstinate and heated with wine, and would not.

The soldiers waited until dark before crossing; in the mean while Jan tried every way to pass the pickets stationed around the fort, but was obliged to give up his idea of rowing over to warn them. He was desperate, but could only sit with De Vreis in the Governor's kitchen and listen, and wait until the midnight silence was broken by the yells and screams of the victims, awakened out of their sleep, but to be murdered by their guardians. Jan walked the floor, or buried his head in a pile of furs; but he never in after life shut out that midnight cry from his mind and heart.

Presently there came to the door some of the Indians who had escaped from their pursuers. As they saw Jan, they said, "We are come here to hide. The Fort Orange Indians are come upon us, and have murdered our wives and little ones." Then Jan, with lips colorless with pain and indignation, said, "No, it is not those you thought were your enemies that have come upon you, it is your friends whom you trusted in. There is no safety for you here."

"Go," said De Vreis, "to the north; and in the darkness of the woods you may find shelter."

"Some of you come with me," said Jan. "We will go out the side door of the fort, while all eyes are fixed upon the Jersey shore, and row over to my cabin; for never will I live here again with these murderers."

The Indians, who had always been so friendly with the Dutch, now arose against them. Jan, through his intimacy with the Canarsies, received first the notice of a plan to revenge the massacre on the Jersey shore, by a complete wiping out of the white settlements. This he quickly told the council in

New Amsterdam. The alarm was sounded.
People residing upon their own boweries, as
well as the poorest trader, flocked to the fort.
All the settlers on Long Island came over,
glad to crowd into a place of comparative
safety. A council of the landholders decided
to send two of their number over to Long
Island to make a treaty with the Indians and
invite them to the fort. Jan was to lead them
to Rockaway, to the camp.

They crossed Sewanachy to the ocean side,
to the camp, where all the chiefs were assembled, dressed in their war paint, sitting in
solemn silence around their speakers. They
placed the three white men in the centre of
the circle, and then the speaker began :

" You pale faces came among us, and we
received you kindly. When you were hungry
we gave you food, fish and corn, and fruits,
and now you turn against us." And taking
out one stick from the many he held in his

hands, he laid it on the ground. He continued, "When you came here we gave you
our daughters for wives, and now you fight
against them." And he laid down another
stick; when De Vreis interrupting him, asked
them to come over to New Amsterdam, and
see the white chief, who would give them
presents. This they agreed to do—when one
of their number arose and said :

"Are you fools, to trust these white men,
when they have deceived you so many
times ?"

Then they hesitated. The chief sachem
raised his hand for silence, and they all sank
back in their seats as rigid and silent as
though hewn out of stone. He beckoned to
Jan to approach, and said :

"Many moons ago we knew your father, and
he was a brave warrior, and your mother the
pale lily; and you we have taught to hunt the
bear with our own sons; and never in your

blood have we found the liar. Tell us what
your chief would have us do ?"

And then, upon Jan's representation, they
went to the fort and made a treaty of peace
with the Dutch.

Jan never broke his vow, never to live
with the Dutch at the fort again. For many
years he lived in his cabin, and became one
of the most famous trappers on the island.
Late in life he married a Huguenot maiden,
who died, leaving him one son, whom he
called Hendrick.

By the time Hendrick was grown and had
married Heleche Poilion, New Amsterdam
was under English rule. They made it a city
and called it New York. Here, a few years
before the Revolution, Hendrick and Hel
eche had become householders ; he was, like
his father, a trapper and hunter, and for weeks
would be away from his family, which consisted of two little girls and Janse, as the boy

was called, after his grandfather, Jan Van Scoy, according to the custom of adding to a name in each generation.

Although New York was a city, it was not like a child's idea of a city.

III.

HEN boys and girls ride in Broadway in an omnibus, and see as far as the eye can reach long rows of splendid buildings, and the street crowded with all sorts of vehicles, they forget it was not always so—that once it was just as much "country" as any village where they may go to spend their summer vacation.

When Janse Van Scoy lived in New York the streets were unpaved roads, with grass fringing their sides, where cows grazed through the summer days.

Along the shore a few ships were loading

or unloading through the summer; but there was no bustle, as in these days.

At the foot of Broadway a battery was built upon the rocks, near the fort and government house, where the British army were quartered. A short distance from these was the "Ferry House," a small frame house with an iron boat and oar over the door for a sign, where the few persons who wanted to cross over the river to the little village of Brooklyn waited for the row-boat to carry them over. Along the green bank of the river, boys sat and fished undisturbed by steamboats, which were then unheard of. Janse lived in a little brick house painted white, standing with gable end to the street, with a sloping thatched roof, projecting over the windows like eyebrows. These windows were made of diamond-shaped panes of glass, set in frames of lead.

The front door was on the side of the

house, and was divided through the centre;
and when the good man of the house chose,
he could close the under half of the door and
rest his arm on the top and talk " low Dutch"
to his neighbors.   But Janse's father was
away hunting the bear, deer and all animals
valuable for their furs, for a rich company,
who sent them across the ocean.   Consequently Janse was the " man of the house"
most of the time.

One afternoon in August, he did not return
home from the Dutch school at the usual
time, but as he was a reliable boy, his mother
was not alarmed about him.   Gretchen, his
sister, had watched for him all the afternoon.
She wanted him to go with her in the woods
back of the house, to gather blackberries to
sell to the soldiers.   She kept her face
pressed close to the window, as long as she
could see the road, and noticed and remarked
to her mother that many of the farmers living

out of town had gone by on horseback. Mrs. Van Scoy had been too much engaged in spinning on the great wheel in the corner, to notice the road; but as twilight came on, she put up her work and stepped out of the back door for wood.

She noticed Hans Hanson, the blacksmith, had covered over the great fire in his shop and left his unfinished work. She mounted the stairs to the garret, and lighted the lantern and hung it on a long pole out of the dormer window to light the street, as was the custom of all householders.

Far down the bowerie she saw groups of persons standing together, and her heart misgave her, for the sound of fife and drum kept always before the people the thought of the oppressive troops and the possible rebellion of the colonists.

Katharine, the youngest child, was lifted up on the high-post bedstead which stood in

3

the corner of the living room. This was piled half way to the ceiling with feather beds, with a deep curtain of blue and white chintz around the top, and a deep valance of the same around the bottom.

At last Janse appeared, heated and excited with running, too full of news to take his bowl of milk and meal which Gretchen had put aside for him.

The ship loaded with tea, which had been so anxiously looked for, had that day arrived. The "Liberty Boys," dressed as Mohawk Indians, were going on board that night to empty the chests of tea into the river. All the people were going down to the wharf to see the fun, and he wanted to return.

Mrs. Van Scoy gave her consent, and he quickly did up the chores; which meant milk the cow and bring in wood from the block under the oak tree.

There were no stoves in those days; a

wide, deep fire-place stretched all across one side of the room ; brass andirons held up the large back logs, under which light wood was placed to start the fire. The boys thought those fire-places hard on the ones who had to prepare the wood they consumed, but rather nice in winter, when they had been skating all the afternoon, to sit in the corner and get warmed through before going up in the cold garret to sleep.

The next day, Saturday, there was no school; business was suspended, church bells rung, guns fired, and all the inhabitants of the town assembled on the "common," where the captain of the vessel in which the tea came over was introduced to the assemblage, the band playing in derision, " God save the Queen." Then the entire populace escorted him to his ship, the " Nancy," which quickly sailed down the bay.

Janse was in the thickest of the crowd.

After the excitement was over, he walked around the British camp, where he was quite a favorite with the soldiers. All the boys in town were well known to them, for they out of school hours brought clams and fish to camp and sold them to the officers.

This afternoon the soldiers were bitter in their denunciation of the inhabitants of the town, and predicted an early retribution ; for the king, they said, had ordered more troops to New York to conquer, in the beginning, the spirit of rebellion.

Janse was only a boy of fourteen, but these stirring times made even boys thoughtful.

This news made him walk quietly home ; even going through the stile, not jumping the fence as was his custom.

The troops, when they came, were to be quartered upon the families in town. He knew his mother, being without a protector, would be compelled to be one of the first to support half a dozen men. This was serious business. Janse knew they had only enough Indian meal to last through the winter, and from the size of the pig in the sty there would be only pork for the four. Should he tell his mother? If his father was only at home! Then he remembered the morning his father left home, when he stood in the wood-shed polishing his gun, that his last words to him were to shield and protect his mother.

His father's sister, Aunt Phebe, lived on a farm on Long Island. He would go to her for advice in the morning. But all was forgotten when he entered the kitchen, and saw " Maniton," his father's trusted Indian messenger and friend, who belonged to the Oneida tribe, and came frequently to New York to exchange furs and maize for blankets and colored beads. As was his wont, Mr. Van Scoy had sent messages of love and greeting, and said that back in the forest they had heard rumors of the colonies uprising ; and if needed, he must join the ranks.

This was sad news to Mrs. Van Scoy, whose father had fought in the Indian wars. When Janse saw how she was saddened, he resolved more firmly to keep evil tidings from her as long as possible. Maniton slept on the garret floor ; he soon disappeared up the stairway, as the ladder was called.

As it was Saturday, Janse had the floor of the living room to sweep and sprinkle with clean beach sand, which it was his pride to wave artistically. It was very nearly Sunday morning before he dropped asleep, after listening to Maniton's stories of battles and bear hunts, with which he always entertained him when they slept in the garret together.

IV.

SUNDAY morning the family attended the Dutch Church, and as the second service was at one o'clock, they ate their lunch of sausages and crullers between services in the church-yard, under the trees.

After Janse had eaten his dinner of cold pork and vegetables (for no fire could be lighted on the Lord's Day), he strolled out in his Sunday clothes, which consisted of high boots, linen breeches to his knees; a round waistcoat, and blue outside coat, and flat broad-brimmed hat.

He walked down the shady lane, and across fields white with buckwheat or waving with grain, to the new English Church of St. Paul, out of town, on the bank of the Hudson River, which some of his military friends had invited him to visit. He took a seat in the organ loft, and looked down on the strange meeting. The clergyman, in his white robe, streaked with the colors of the stained glass windows; the radiance of the western sun lighting up the steps of the pulpit ; the breeze swaying the leaves of the trees outside, and the font beneath him filled with flowers rare and sweet, whose perfume floated up to him, forming part of the service of that afternoon. The music of the organ sounded soft and low through the church. The choir sang the "Gloria," "Thou that takest away the sins of the world have mercy upon us." Higher and higher arose the sweet voices, until Janse was filled with awe. He thought he must be very near the city that his mother read to him of out of the old iron-clasped Bible brought by his grandfather from France. It was a service he would never forget; his French extraction made him appreciate it.

Monday, Janse went down to the officer of the day and received a pass to leave the city. He then went to the market place, where the farmers from Long Island stood with their wagons of grain and vegetables for sale. He soon found one of his Uncle Seaman's neighbors, who would return home that afternoon. Janse met him at noon at the old " Inn." On the long wooden stoop farmers were sitting after their dinner. Overhead, suspended from an apple tree in front of the house, was the sign—a brilliant picture of King George.

Janse climbed into the wagon and went over the river to Brooklyn in a sloop; row-boats only carrying foot passengers.

All the way up, as they passed little cabins

by the road side, anxious women came out to
inquire the latest news. Not one flinched
in their determination to stand firm, at what-
ever cost, in their resistance to oppression.

Janse dropped asleep to the sound of the
crickets, only to awaken at Uncle Seaman's
door. Aunt Phebe brought him a bowl of warm
milk and brown bread ; then left him to finish
his nap on the broad "settle" in the kitchen,
until the household had retired for the night;
when closing doors and windows, they listened to his earnest words, and decided to send
down the large wagon and bring them all up
to the farm without explaining the reason.
Uncle Seaman was a Quaker, and connected
with General Howe's family ; consequently he
was free from British molestation.

Mrs. Van Scoy was shocked and alarmed
next day, when Uncle Seaman and Janse
arrived with the wagon. She, with many
others, hoped against hope ; although all

events pointed to a rebellion against the
mother country. The simple folk thought
something would occur to prevent it; so
she left her home as for a visit, thinking
in a few weeks to return, but very glad of the
shelter and protection of Uncle Seaman's
influence.

The morning after their arrival at the farm
Janse and Gretchen went to the cabin they
were to occupy, swept out the dead leaves,
hung the door with straps of leather for
hinges, put up the " slapbank," which looked
like a cupboard with closed doors, through
the day, and was lowered at night for a bed.
Janse slept in the garret. The long-handled
warming-pan, filled with lighted wood, he
thought would make his bed very comfortable, if the cracks between the logs in the
roof did let the snow in.

All the autumn there were mutterings of
discontent; but as yet there were no decided

steps taken; only the sense of wrong was deepening, and preparations were being made for the inevitable result.

Janse and Gretchen roamed the woods, bringing home baskets of black walnuts and hickory nuts, to store in a corner of the garret, where, upon stormy days, they sat with a basket of apples before them to be pared, cut in slices, and strung on long cords suspended from the rafters to dry for winter use. Janse used to, in the long days when their mother was busy at the farm-house, take his rifle and shoot game for Gretchen to cook.

Janse was short and stout, a regular Hollander; but Gretchen was tall and slim, the French blood of her mother's family predominating in her. In the bottom of a heavily bound chest was a miniature of their great grandmother, a Huguenot exile, who had fled from France to Staten Island for religious liberty. Often when their mother returned from Aunt

Phebe's, and Katharine was asleep, they would sit in the fire-light and listen to her stories of her grandfather's flight from Paris, that sad St. Bartholomew's eve, until they could almost hear the great bell ring out the signal for the midnight massacre. It grew with their life, until it became part of their daily thoughts—the sublime idea of personal sacrifice for principle.

When the snow barricaded their door, and for several days prevented their mother returning to them or their leaving the house, they would remind each other of the crowded vessel their grandfather came over in.

All through the spring of '76, the colonists were preparing to cut loose from the British government. General Washington had been made Commander-in-chief of the army, and had possession of New York. Congress was sitting in the State House at Philadelphia, where on the fourth of July, the Declaration of Independence was signed.

Janse's father had joined the army, and was stationed somewhere in the vicinity of New York; but as they had not heard directly from him, they knew not the regiment to which he was attached.

V.

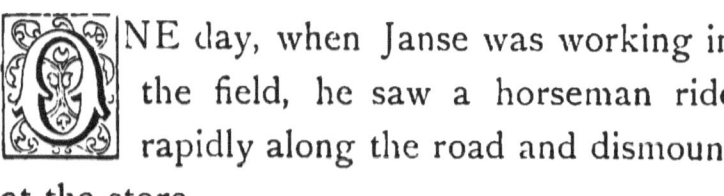

NE day, when Janse was working in the field, he saw a horseman ride rapidly along the road and dismount at the store.

In those exciting days all thought was centered on the army. Janse, knowing how anxious his mother was for news, quickly wended his way to the spot, where all the men in the place were in a short space of time congregated. The soldier, who was a messenger sent from Brooklyn, quickly explained his errand. The enemy had landed on Long Island, ten thousand strong, and all men capable of doing military duty were to report immediately to the Continental Army at Brooklyn.

Janse ran home that sultry afternoon to beg his mother to let him go and look for his father. He was too young to be regularly enrolled, but Mrs. Van Scoy consented to his going as a drummer-boy.

Around the " tavern " all the villagers were assembled when Janse rejoined the throng. The men marched down the road, led by the drum beaten so lustily by Janse, leaving the tearful, sorrowful women behind them, who kept up bravely until the turn of the road hid the men from sight ; when they returned to their homes in the late afternoon, to go themselves to the pasture and drive home the cattle, and prepare to gather in the harvest ripened in the fields.

The sun went before the company of men as they marched westward. At almost every farm one or more joined them, carrying the guns their fathers or grandfathers had used in the Indian wars. At twilight they stopped at a low stone house for the man who was to lead them into Brooklyn. Their hostess took them into the kitchen, and placed before them rye bread, boiled beef and cabbage; but the men were too excited to eat. As for Janse, the march had been a perfect delight to him.

The unusual sound of fife and drum awoke the echoes in the hills and valleys they crossed. The deer and squirrel bounded before them as they passed stone fences covered with wild vines. Ofttimes he would forget, and stop to gather the wild grapes hanging before him; but no, behind him came the steady tramp of determined men—he must keep drumming on. It was midnight when they reached Jamaica, where they were to halt. Tired and footsore, they lay down on the clean hay in the barn, where, notwithstanding the increased excitement, Janse sank to sleep.

All night farmers arrived from the sur-rounding country. Whig families came in from Brooklyn with all their possessions, feather beds, Dutch dresses, and babies all huddled together. Officers were coming and going with orders from General Sullivan. By daylight the word of march was given. A motley crowd—gray-haired men and mere striplings, marched side by side, each dressed in his farm clothes, buckskin trousers and striped shirt. A range of hills stretched along back of Brooklyn. Between each range a roadway led through the passes. Unfortunately, the regiment which had been placed at the passes to guard the breastworks had been withdrawn, leaving them exposed to the enemy. Just as Janse's company reached the army, they were ordered directly down to the river pass, on the ground now occupied by Greenwood Cemetery.

The battle had commenced. In the thickest of the fight, Janse's drum was heard cheering his men on. Before them was the trained rank and file of the British army. Company after company were driven back into the shadow of the hills. They had either to surrender or cut their way through the British soldiery. This seemed impossible. The main body of the army withdrew as best they could. They would rather sink in the meadow around them than surrender. Five times, four hundred Marylanders charged upon the British, covering their friends' retreat. Each time they were repulsed, until they were obliged to submit and be taken prisoners.

Janse had fallen where the first stand was made. Slowly, late in the afternoon, he opened his eyes. All around him was quiet,

only the quail telling its mate, "Wheat's
ripe." The corn waved and sang its requiem
ovef the dead beyond it, where the battle had
been fought. The wild flowers, pressed by
the tramp of many feet, still breathed per-
fumes from their crushed hearts.

Janse was lying alone—only a boy—and
the world so bright before him. If he had
only found his father he would have been
content. He raised his head and saw the
sun sinking into the waters of the bay. Was
his life going down with it? "O mother,
mother, in the land beyond the sea, shall I
meet you again?"

Beyond the band was playing—the music
in the distance, sounding as soft and sweet to
him as it did that Sunday afternoon in the
English Church in New York, which appeared as a vision before him. The perfume
of the flowers, and the music, brought it all
back to him. And the words the choir sang,

"Thou that takest away the sins of the world, have mercy upon us." With these words upon his lips he sank back and was gone.

Just then the party which had been sent out to reconnoitre for the wounded, came through the field, and seeing the boy, so young and fair, with one arm shattered, picked him up in their strong arms and carried him into camp, intending to send his body back to his mother, or at least give him a decent burial; but they found his heart still beating, and gave him into the hands of the surgeon, who had only time to give him stimulants as he hurried through the rooms of the "Old Cortelyou House" they had converted into a hospital. There Janse, lulled by opiates, dozed through the night and next day, scarcely noticing the surroundings, until the order came to remove the wounded nearer the East River.

O the torture of that ride in the farmer's

wagon, over the rough road! Janse soon
fainted with pain, and remained unconscious
until dark, when the fine mist falling on his
face revived him. Gradually the moisture
penetrated to his inflamed limb, making it
feel more comfortable. They were at the
ferry, preparing to embark on the long row-
boats waiting to carry them over. General
Washington had been in camp and hospital
all day. Now he was in the saddle superin-
tending the removal from the ferry stairs,
the present Fulton Ferry. Patiently all
night the General waited through the rain,
as the tired boatmen rowed back and forth
across the river.

The British camp was wrapped in slumber,.
secure in their victory ; but when daylight
appeared, imagine their surprise to see the
whole Continental army safely landed on the
New York shore.

Janse was quartered with a family living

on the shore road. Kind hands ministered
unto him, the women of the house nursing
him, and trying to soothe his home-sickness.
He was soon able to walk around. Uncle
Seaman procured him a pass to go around
the town. The American army had retreated
into Westchester, and the British had pos-·
session of New York.

As soon as he was able, he visited his old
home. Opposite the house a narrow bridge
crossed the little river, which ran before the
door where he had often sat and fished. The
unfinished boats were still upon the stocks
before the closed boat-house. He stopped
to take a drink out of the old bucket in the
well. Up the dusty road was neighbor
Smith's house and barn; beyond stood De
Witt's windmill, its long arms revolving with
the wind. Before it stood a long wagon,
loaded with bags of grain for the army. He
wondered if he should ever live there again,

for he was to leave next day for home; he could hardly sleep that night for anticipation.

Very glad was he to get home and rest upon his own garret bed. Every day the neighbors came in to see him and talk over the battle. Five of the men who left the village with him had never returned from that hill-pass, and Janse resolved as soon as he was perfectly well he would search the battle-field for some token of the lost ones, particularly of his father, that his mother's mind might be relieved of the suspense which was wearing her life out. She was most of the time at Uncle Seaman's with Gretchen and Katharine. Gretchen was as a daughter in the house, Uncle Seaman taking as much pride in her and indulging her as far as his Quaker principles would allow him. Having no children of his own, he had made his will in favor of Mrs. Van Scoy's children.

The house he lived in, the "Big House,"

was half a mile from the cabin; a two-story double house, with four windows each side of the front door, with a broad veranda across the front. The hall through the centre was as wide as an ordinary house. On one side was the living rooms and kitchen, on the other, the best room gloried in an oriental rug spread upon its oiled floor, with heavy mahogany furniture, and a looking-glass with black and gilt frame, surmounted with a gilded eagle.

Aunt Norchie was too good a house-keeper to have the negroes under her feet in the house; only old Dinah and her reliable daughter had permanent possession there; the rest of the tribe lived in white-washed cabins back of the house. In Uncle Seaman's desk was safely locked the freedom papers of all the negroes on the place. He, as a Quaker, could not keep any human being in bondage, but they lived on the place the same as before he bought it, and they with it.

" Janse, thee will have to take the milk to friend Jones' this afternoon," said Aunt Phebe, one afternoon, when he had been home a few weeks.

" All right!" And he took the kettle of milk and started to go a couple of miles out of the village. He walked along, careful of the milk, and thinking of the conversation they had in the barn that afternoon. Cæsar and Dinah had been telling the children of witches, as they sat upon the barn floor husking corn, until the wool had almost straightened upon Sam and Dan's black heads ; they believed everything " Mammy " said. That Jennie, the cow, had been bewitched in the summer, when the supply of milk had failed. In fact everything was regulated by surrounding witches.

Gretchen's black eyes had snapped in

scorn, but while Janse had laughed with her, in his secret soul there was a little uneasiness, for in their household, Uncle Seaman's grandmother's name was never mentioned but with sadness, for she had been burned as a witch in Boston. He thought, after all, there might be some truth in Dinah's stories.

"Well, good-night, Janse," said Israel Jones. "We'll have an early moon to-night," as Janse at last picked up his empty pail and turned his face homeward; he had been so interested in Israel's arrangements for a deer hunt, that he had not noticed how late it was. He whistled through one piece of woods until he came to the big walnut tree, standing alone on the shore of the lake; this he stopped to shake until he had filled his pockets with nuts, transferring a great piece of warm molasses cake to the kettle. He didn't feel hungry just then; he took it from Mrs. Jones more to please her than anything else.

While he stood there he heard some one
singing, "As pants the heart for cooling
streams—cooling streams—cooling streams."
He knew at once who it was—Crazy Jack;
but he was perfectly harmless, roaming the
country at will, although he had a good home
in the village.

"Good evening, sir," said Janse, in his most
respectful manner.

"Good evening, Janse; been nutting?"

"Yes, sir; have some?"

"Guess not." And he passed along, still
singing, "Cooling streams."

Janse thought he had better hurry home.
It was already twilight, as he walked fast
along the shore, and entered another wood
lot. After that came the bridge, and the
orchard, and then he would be at home. He
had gone a quarter of a mile through the
woods, when he thought he heard a rustling
in the bushes. There were plenty of wild-

cats and wolves in the woods, but they seldom came near the road. He listened, and distinctly heard steps behind him. His heart stood still; he listened again, and all was quiet; he tried to whistle, but his voice died away, for again he heard a rustling sound. It must be the witches! He started and ran as fast as his weakness permitted; the lid of the kettle flew off and clattered behind him. At last he stopped to rest—he was so weak— when he heard some one calling " Midnight !" And as it was a human voice, his courage returned, for he knew it must be a friend who knew one of the passwords of the American army.

He hesitated; what should he do? Go home, or go back through that dreadful woods, he had filled with imaginary hob-goblins? How Gretchen would despise him, if she knew he had thought a ghost was after him! He slowly retraced his steps, peering

into the gathering darkness, when he heard
a voice repeat again, " Midnight !"

" Yes, and darkness," replied Janse.

" Is that Janse Van Scoy ?"

" Yes."

Immediately Janse was relieved to feel his
hand grasped by another strong one, made
of flesh and blood, as a tall man, wrapped in
a long cape, stepped out of the woods.

"I have been waiting for you all day.   I
have a message for your Uncle Seaman.   Is
it safe to talk here, Janse ?"

"I don't know; but it is safe in the bear cave
on the hill.   No one goes there but us boys."

" Well, lead the way.   I must find a place
of safety."

It was now quite dark, but Janse knew
every step of the way ; the man followed, and
Janse, taking him by the hand, led him into
the mouth of the cave, where bears had once
been shot.

"Have you come far?" asked Janse.

"Yes, and I have been in the woods all day."

"Then you must be hungry, sir?"

"Yes; but I am content to bear all hardships if I can accomplish my mission."

Janse thought, before any more was said, he had better get out his gingerbread and nuts, which he was made happy by seeing this gentleman eat. Then crouching close together, on the bottom of the cave, they soon understood each other. Janse loved, from the moment he saw the moonlight upon it, the face of Nathan Hale, so strong and sweet. It aroused all the ardor in Janse's soul to look into those deep earnest eyes, as they kindled with the story of his country's wrongs, and grew humid when he spoke of General Washington's confidence in him, in selecting him to come to Long Island to find out the strength of the British army. He had received his instructions from the General at the house of Robert Murray, a Quaker in New York, who had told him he would find a friend in Joshua Seaman.

But while he spoke of the honor of doing this, he did not mention that in volunteering for this secret mission, he was hazarding his life. He did not appear to think of himself, only of his country, and how he might best serve her. Janse could not stay any longer ; his long absence might arouse suspicion. He promised to return as soon as possible, and hastened home.

"Thee is late, Janse," said Aunt Phebe, when he reached home ; " the table is cleared, but Dinah will find thee something."

He had no doubt on that score. The larder was always filled to overflowing.

" I'se awful glad to see you again, Massa Janse ; thought for sure the spookes had yer ; jist the night they ride on broomsticks."

"O come, Dinah, I can run as fast as spookes; give me something—a whole pie; I'm as hungry as a coon."

He cut a small piece out and slipped the rest under the lounge, while Dinah's back was turned.

"Come now give me some cheese."

"'Clar to man, Massa Janse, I neber seed such eatin' in all my born days! Hull pie gone jist while I was fixin' Massa's flip."

"Better give me some bread, then."

But Dinah had gone into the hall, muttering, "Sure 'nuff, the witches have got him; he's witched, for sure."

Janse cracked nuts all the evening, sitting in the chimney corner listening to Uncle Seaman's dignified attempts to teach the colored twins to read; while they kept one eye on Massa, and one on Janse, who occasionally threw them a nut. But all the time his mind was with Nathan Hale, in the cave on the

5

hill-side. He thought the evening would never go; but that, like all things, came to an end. The servants were called in, Uncle Seaman had prayers, and the fire was covered up, the lamps put out, and the house was quiet.

Janse retired to his own room, threw himself on the bed without removing his clothes, but only to listen for the last sound to die out of the house. Then he crept down to the broad staircase, with his shoes in his hand, to Uncle Seaman's private room, where he generally sat for an hour or two after the rest had retired, arranging his business for the next day.

He heard with deep sympathy, Janse's story, and sat a moment in profound thought. He read the letter from General Washington, asking him to befriend Captain Nathan Hale, who was on secret service.

" Janse," he said, "he must not stay there

until morning—it is not safe. But thee cannot go again. Thee is not able ; I will go
myself, and thee stay here until I return."

" But, uncle, you cannot go ; it is steep
climbing, that hill."

" Dost thee think thy old uncle too stiff,
Janse, to climb the hills I was brought up
in ?"

" I can go, uncle. I am not tired."

" Nay, nay, Janse, sit thee down quietly
in my arm-chair, and wait until I return, and
when I tap on the window, open it."

Janse extinguished the candle, and opened
the window, out of which Uncle Seaman
stepped on the lawn. Then burying his head
in his arms upon the table, he watched and
waited, listening to the tall clock in the hall.
When it chimed the second quarter, a slight
step was perceptible outside ; then the tap on
the window, and Janse opened it to admit
Uncle Seaman and Captain Hale. Then clos-

ing the wooden shutters and relighting the
candle, he departed for food and drink for
their visitor.

After Captain Hale had been refreshed and
strengthened with sufficient food, he unfolded
his plans to Friend Seaman. That scene
Janse never forgot. That small room, with
low dark rafters overhead, the blue painted
doors and window, the old chest of drawers
with brass rings and knobs, with a desk top
before, where Uncle Seaman sat, with his
eyes fixed upon the paper before him, upon
which Captain Hale was tracing his route of
return to Huntington, where he was to take a
sloop to go down the East River to the
American headquarters.

He had been successful in obtaining all the
information desired, and now, elated, was returning full of enthusiasm and zeal. They
were a marked contrast. Uncle Seaman's
calm pale face, made even more so by the

straight drab coat buttoned to the throat.
Captain Hale wore a butternut colored cloth
suit, with a ruffled shirt bosom, his hair powdered and tied in a queue down his back,
his cheeks flushed with excitement; a grand
type of manhood, Janse thought, as he knelt
on the bags of seed close by Uncle Seaman,
and rested; in his way as much interested as
they, for he knew the cuts through the
hills better than either. It was early morning before they separated. Janse taking Captain Hale to his room until Uncle Seaman
could decide what was best to do.

VI.

THE next day Janse was too ill to come down to breakfast. Aunt Phebe brought his breakfast to his room, the quantity of which only confirmed Dinah in her conviction of his being bewitched. Through the day enough was smuggled into the room to keep one person a week. It was thought best for Janse to remain in bed the next day also, which was Saturday.

Sunday morning the long wagon painted drab, was brought out by Janse, the bottom filled with straw and robes. Mrs. Van Scoy and Aunt Phebe sat on the back seat. Uncle Seaman and Janse in front. As soon as

they were out of sight of the servants, the fur
robes were removed from the bottom of the
wagon, and disclosed Captain Hale, extended
the whole length of the wagon. The covering was again placed over him, as they
approached the meeting house and met
Friends coming from different directions.

The men sat one side of the building, the
women the other. The walls were white-
washed, the windows without blinds. On a
raised pine platform sat the speakers, chief
among whom was Uncle Seaman. Janse sat
by a window where he could keep his eye
upon the wagon. It was what they called
"Silent Meeting." Grave and motionless sat
the men in drab, with broad brimmed hats on
their heads. Grave and motionless sat the
women, in drab, with close drab bonnets upon
their heads—only the singing of the birds
and buzzing of the bees outside, praising God
in that still air. The Spirit did not move any

of the Friends to speak through the long morning, until noon, when one Friend turning to another, they all through the room began to shake hands, and then the meeting was over.

Janse brought the wagon up to the door, but the rest had decided to remain at a Friend's house, where a celebrated Friend who had "a concern to testify," would speak in the afternoon.

Uncle Seaman said Janse had better drive home for Cæsar, and proceed from thence to New York for a load of salt. Janse's arm was still too weak to allow him to drive any distance. This occasioned no surprise, for frequently the Quakers went to meeting in the morning, and in the field to work in the afternoon. Janse drove home and found Cæsar, who drove a mile down the road to where another joined it, and then, as he was let into the secret, turned up the new road along the shore, and went five miles east; Captain Hale, sitting on the seat with Janse, telling him stories of his own boyhood and farm life, for he was brought up on a farm in Connecticut, until he went to College. There Captain Hale left them to go into the woods until night allowed him to wait upon the shore at Huntington for the sloop which was to take him to New York.

It was late in the afternoon when they drove into Peter Remson's yard at Brooklyn, but Janse was soon at home, smoking his pipe and talking low Dutch. Early the next morning he went over to the city, with his pass in his pocket, that he might go in and out among the British soldiers and pick up bits of news, and learn whether a sloop had gone up the Hudson River. He was anxious to know if the sloop which had left Huntington with Captain Hale had arrived, as they had a fair wind through the night.

Not *that* one had arrived, but alas! another—a British vessel lying at Huntington the night before, sent a small boat to the land, and Captain Hale, thinking it was the one in quest of him, hailed it, and was taken on board only to find out his fatal mistake. He was searched. The charts and papers found upon him disclosed all. He was brought directly to New York, and given in charge of the Provost, the cruel, inhuman Cunningham, who had placed him under guard, in the green house, on the very ground where he had received his directions from General Washington, who had left the city almost directly after—the British General occupying the Murray mansion, on what is now called Murray Hill.

This Janse learned from the British soldiers. His knees smote together. He forgot all about Cæsar and the salt. He only thought of going to Captain Hale. He knew where the place was; but he dare not be seen around in the daylight; he must wait until dark. He sauntered around the city, watching the boys fish in the Collect.

In the twilight Janse reconnoitered the grounds. He found a soldier patrolling the front of the green house, but nothing in the rear, where close by a window grew a large beech tree. Janse clambered up in that, the thick foliage hiding him in the gathering darkness.

" Captain Hale," he said, in a low, distinct whisper.

" Janse, can it be you here ?"

" Yes, sir."

" You have done me the greatest and last kindness you ever can, Janse. It does not seem so hard now that I have one friend by me. Cunningham will not allow me a candle, or paper, or ink."

" I have a piece of paper and a pencil."

By the light of the full moon Janse threw
them into the room, and there, by the light of
that harvest moon, Nathan Hale wrote his
last message to his friends, quietly sleeping
far away in their home in the Connecticut
Valley. Then reaching his hand out the
window, he gave the message to Jan, who
promised to deliver it himself. He was
ready to promise anything that could comfort
his friend, who stood looking out on the
quiet lovely view before him — the hay
ricks, standing like sentinels in the field;
the moonlight so bright that everything was
distinctly visible—even the apples glistened
on the trees. The warm breeze swayed
the honeysuckle which covered the garden
house — the myriad stars above in the sky
so clear. He looked at the stars; then
sinking on his knees at the window he buried
his face in his hands. Janse's heart was broken with grief for his friend, and his tears

fell like rain on the leaves around him. A
great sob broke from him, when Captain
Hale said :

"Janse."

"Sir !"

"It must be nearly morning ; you must go
now."

"I can't go."

"I wan't you to. It will not be long now.
The sunrise will soon be here ; already there
are light streaks in the east."

"I cannot leave you ;" and Janse held on
convulsively to the hand stretched out to
him. He could not speak, as Captain Hale
said musingly, "You will see the old school-
house. Tell my mother I died loving her,
and to send the message of my death across
the mountains to the little brown cottage.
Janse, you must go. I must do my part
bravely, and you, yours. We will meet
again one day."

"Good-bye."

Janse hid himself until the guard of sol
diers arrived, with the portly Cunningham,
brilliant in gold trimmings, who refused
Nathan Hale's last request for a clergymen,
and ordered him to march down to Rutger's
orchard, now East Broadway. Firmly and
erect he looked the insolent minion calmly in
the face, and replied to his taunts:

" I regret I have but one life to give to my
country."

Firmly he walked, until they reached the
apple tree from which a rope was suspended.
Janse had a full view of that pale, heroic
man, with his eyes fixed on the light
which illumined his face, until he could
look no more, but throwing himself down on
the grass he shook with uncontrollable sobs.
He heard Cunningham's voice giving orders.
Then a silence.

The soldiers and populace soon moved,

but Janse dared not raise his head until all had departed, and only the sound of apples dropping around him proved that he was alone. Then he went and stood by the hastily covered grave, and felt as if his heart must burst. It was his first grief, and his strong, though young nature, felt it more acutely than an older and more disciplined one would.

Then slowly walking down town, he reached the ferry, which he crossed. His shoulders pained him extremely; he was feverish and exhausted with his long night watch in the open air; but he could not rest. The paper carefully pinned inside his shirt bosom impelled him onward. He took pas-,sage on a sloop across the Sound, and then walked the rest of the way to Coventry, stopping at the log houses he passed for food, which was gladly given him in return for the information he imparted.

Sunday morning he reached the village

The quietness in the houses he passed, and
the line of horses in the church yard, showed
him that the whole village was at meeting.
Tired and footsore he walked the dusty road ;
then sitting down beneath a tree, he waited
for the congregation to return to their homes.
He watched the brook softly trickling over
the stones, just washing the rushes by its
side, then flowing down to the mill whose
wheel it turned.   Slowly and decorously the
people came out of the " meeting house."
Women, with a few old men.   One tall, thin
man came up to Janse, and said :

" Do you know this is the Sabbath day ?"

" Yes, sir," replied Janse, looking up with
astonishment.   There was no question about
it in his mind ; every latch-string was drawn
in, and every child, even, in meeting. · The
way the boys walked down the road two by
two, never turning their heads even to look at
Janse who stood in their path ; the very birds

in a New England town appeared to keep
the Sabbath day.

" Do you not know that it is not lawful to
travel on the Sabbath day ? Have you no
abiding place ?"

" Yes, sir ; but I want to find Mrs. Hale."

" What do you want her for ? She has
just gone home from the meeting."

" I want to tell her that her son is dead,"
and Janse's voice shook.

" What, Captain Nathan Hale killed in
battle !"

" No, sir ;" and here Janse broke down, and
fainted from hunger and exhaustion. Quickly
his questioner picked him up, and carried
him over to Mrs. Hale's, which fortunately
was near.

They laid him on the high-post bedstead,
and gave him rum and sugar to revive him,
then left him to sleep until the sun went down,
and the Sabbath day in Connecticut was fin-

ished.   The neighbors came in and prepared
the evening meal.   Mrs. Hale and her
daughters were not allowed to assist; they
sat weeping in the best room.

Then all sat quietly around the room
until the minister came in, dressed in black,
his hair powdered and tied in a queue down
his back.   For a few moments there was perfect silence, and then, at a motion from the
minister, they dropped upon their knees, and
joined in thought with his words.   " Lord,
Thou hast been our refuge in all generations."
Then rising to their seats, Janse, amid the
sobs of the women, told all he knew of Nathan Hale's capture and death.   Then the
minister read his last letter aloud.

After the first grief was spent, the usual
quietness and resignation was restored.   Not
one of those women, but had sent one loved
one at least to the army.   Any day they
might hear the same tidings of their death,

but they had no wish to recall them. Too much was at stake. Their children and their homes, the farms their fathers had redeemed from the wilderness — all — all called upon them to be brave.

That stricken household was very kind to Janse—putting him in "Brother Nathan's" room to sleep. For several days he was so weak and ill, he could only wander around the farm, and sleep in the hay in the barn. They wanted him to spend some weeks with them, but he wanted to go home to his mother. His nervous system was completely exhausted. His nights were disturbed by dreams of that terrible scene in Rutger's orchard.

They let him depart with blessings and tears, riding on their old white horse, attended by a neighbor's boy, who was to bring the horse back ; when Janse took the boat for Long Island, and the next day reached home.

VII.

IN November was the annual sacrifice of swine in the barn-yard. In the "out kitchen," immense iron pots of head-cheese, meat and lard, hung over the fire. In the great store-room were hung long links of sausage and hams. One upper room was filled to the ceiling with wool and flax to be carded, spun and wove into blankets and cloth for winter use.

They must have expected a very severe winter, from the quantity of blankets made and rolls of cloth dyed butternut and blue for men's wear, locked up in the closet. Uncle Seaman's best suit of clothes was drab broad-

cloth, and cloak of camlet. Aunt Phebe's best
cloak and hat were of black satin.

It was an Indian summer afternoon. Over
the hills the cows were coming home, driven
by black Sam. The chickens were quietly
going to roost in the trees. Carlo was
asleep in the sun. Aunt Phebe had driven
over to see a sick friend. The men with the
children, both black and white, were down in
the far orchard gathering the late apples.
The house was alone. On the dresser in the
kitchen were the fresh loaves of wheat and
rye bread, rows of pumpkin and apple pies,
and great piles of doughnuts and crullers.

The floor was scoured white. Through
the open door the old oak threw an occa-
sional leaf with its shadows. On a hook in
the deep, broad fireplace hung the copper
tea kettle, singing away, and bright enough
for Dinah to see her face in. The hour-glass

stood on the shelf with its sands slowly but steadily running through.

Janse came up from the orchard with a load of red and green fruit, and climbed up on the top of the cider house to arrange a place for them, when his notice was attracted by an unusual sight on the Sound. A large vessel was at anchor, and landing a number of men. He soon distinguished the green coat faced with red, and the red and drab cap of the Hessians, the terror of the country. His first impulse was to warn his uncle ; but he could not run ; he was too weak, and the enemy were steadily marching up the road.

He went in at the back door of the house, and ran up to the corner room where the silver pint mug and spoons were kept, and buried them under the feather beds; then walked to the front gate as the soldiers approached the house. Already one of them had driven the cows out of the yard, while another had mounted the load of apples Janse had left standing. When he said that his uncle was a Quaker, and under British protection, they laughed at him.

He took down the tin horn, used to call the men in to dinner from the fields, and blew a blast which could be heard a mile away. In a few minutes Uncle Seaman appeared with his wagon load of assistants, and satisfied the commanding officer that his house was neutral ground, and invited them to dine with him.

Aunt Norchie returned, and Janse went for his mother, for Dinah could not be left alone in the kitchen. The sight of a " green coat " in the door or at the well, filled her with dismay. Turkeys and chickens were prepared by her for roasting in the brick oven. Uncle Seaman was lavish in his hospitality, for he knew they dared not plunder his barn or house as they would his less in–

fluential neighbors, whom he wished to spare.

The long table was laid in the hall with queensware and pewter. Dozens of wine were brought out of the cellar. A hogshead of shad, salted down for winter use, was prepared, and in the woods oxen were killed and roasted whole for the common soldiers, who helped themselves to the cider already made. By midnight all were satisfied and ready to begin their march to the place of encampment. five miles beyond, where they were to remain all winter.

In the morning the yard and fields looked as though a hurricane had passed over them, so completely was the grass trodden down and the fences destroyed for fire-wood. The officers made arrangements with Uncle Seaman to provide their table with milk and butter, and guaranteed his safety from foraging parties.

The farmers around them suffered severe-ly that winter. Pigs and chickens were kept in the cellars, fire-wood was kept under beds. None could be left outside with safety. The women and children left at home, were pow-erless to oppose the demands of a party of soldiers, who drove away the cows they depended upon. A child would sit by an open window and keep watch up and down the road while the mother ran to the well for water.

One day Gretchen, attended by black Sam, went to the camp with milk. The soldiers surrounded her as she stood blushing, in her red cloak and hood, until the officer of the day appeared, and took her under his pro-tection as the men slunk away. Never after-wards was she spoken to, in her journeys to camp with Sam. She returned one after-noon in a heavy storm, which drenched her thoroughly. In the morning she tried to

appear bright at breakfast, but her head
ached badly.   She did not speak of it before
her mother left.

In the evening, when Mrs. Van Scoy
returned, she found Gretchen very ill with
fever.   She undressed her, and Janse sat
beside her, cooling her hot hands with cold
water.   All night her mother went outside
when she, in her delirium, called for ice, and
gathered the snow to put to her hot lips.
Once she leaned against a tree by the door,
and looked up through the frosty air at the
stars, and listened to the wolves in the forest.
This night her courage failed her.   She had
not heard from her husband in months.
Gretchen so ill, so far from medical skill, and
no one to share her long vigil .but Janse.
How her heart brightened when she thought
of her strong, brave boy.

When Aunt Norchie came over in the
morning, they decided to send him ten miles

to the Indian settlement to a medicine man there. Janse found him in his wigwam, stretched upon a pile of furs. Black-haired children rolled upon the ground. The squaw sat in the door-way, with a long wrap of skins around her, beautifully trimmed with wild grasses and ferns sewed upon it. Janse was so anxious about Gretchen, he hurried home as rapidly as possible.

The next day she was still more delirious, and Aunt Norchie even became discouraged. Janse said he would go down to the beach, and see if there was any vessel going to New York, that he might go and consult their old physician. He found one boat ready to start, but the crew demurred about taking him, until Captain Jones appeared, whom he had often met at Uncle Seaman's. He spoke to the crew aside, and then said Janse might come down in the afternoon to sail with them.

It was late when the sloop sailed. To
Janse it was delightful, although it was
rather cold when the spray dashed over him.
The sloop cut its way bravely through the
waters. He fell asleep by midnight, and was
awakened by loud voices beside him. The
sloop was at anchor in the middle of the
Sound, beside another vessel without lights,
to which they were transferring their cargo.

For a few minutes Janse was dazed ; then
slowly he comprehended the situation, as he
saw several barrels from Uncle Seaman's
store-room carried out of the hold. The
Captain explained the whole situation to him,
for he said Uncle Seaman had said Janse was
to be trusted.

A vessel awaited them at a given spot on
the Sound, which conveyed their cargo of
produce and clothing to the American army.
All along the Island, people were aiding, in
this way, their starving, freezing friends, as

their poverty would allow. Few were as
rich as Uncle Seaman. In the early morning they passed through Hell Gate, a dangerous bed of rocks in the East River, well
known to the sailors around New York.

They saw a large British vessel coming
behind them over the dangerous rocks. The
Captain watched it with interest. He and
his crew were too familiar with those waters
to dash through as recklessly as the British
Captain was doing. It was but a moment, till
she ran upon a large rock, which stove a hole
through her bottom. She sank rapidly.
Part of the crew jumped and swam to the
sloop ; then she sank to the bottom with an
immense amount of gold to the bed of the
river, where they have lain one hundred years.

Janse was ready to return with the sloop
that same evening. When they again
reached the trysting place on the waters, they
met a vessel at anchor, to which they con-

veyed the guns and ammunition sent by friends from New York.

Janse gave his mother the medicine for Gretchen, which relieved her immediately. In a few days she was able to taste the fruit, and look at the English picture papers Captain Lushington sent to her from camp to amuse her and Katharine, while their mother was at the big house.

Janse was not strong enough for much work that summer. He was generally seen early in the morning, starting for the woods, with his gun upon his shoulder, or with old Cæsar, out on the bay in his boat, although it was noticed that he never brought any result of his labors back with him. The black boys on the place thought "Massa Janse hab easy times," and offered to go with him to row the boat, but he always declined. They didn't see the roll of cloth or linen under Janse's jacket.

He was a good marksman, and often carried a boat load of wild ducks to the cave under the hill, where the Captain of the sloop found them at night. He would leave Cæsar in the boat below the cliff, take his gun and reconnoitre the vicinity before he signalled him to land. If he met foraging parties out from camp, they laughed at his idle life, without suspecting the truth.

Janse was an energetic, ambitious boy. His cheeks would flush hotly when he met any of his poor neighbors, hard worked women carrying their little " garden sass " to the store to exchange for articles of necessity, when he apparently was playing his life away. But when he met Captain Jones of the sloop, who told him of the half naked, half starved men in the army, who blessed him for food and clothing, he would resolve to work harder to keep his rocky store-room constantly replenished through the summer.

Cæsar had learned the trade of shoemak-
ing in his youth, and as much as he remembered he taught Janse. All through the
next fall, as the evenings grew longer, they
were in an upper room, with a thick blanket
pinned before the window, making shoes,
coarse and clumsy to be sure; but thick and
warm, which found their way in time to the
cave, that a few, at least, of the men, who the
winter before tracked the snow with their
feet frozen and bloody, might be more comfortable.

Back in the country faithful hearts beat for
the absent ones. They heard of the battles
between the British and Americans, as month
after month rolled on. The women and
children had almost forgotten what it was
to have a man to work and care for
them.

The children were learning to forget their
father's face. They had grown like Janse

from childhood to manhood. His mother at last consented to his going down to Brooklyn to learn a trade at the mill at Walla-bout.

VIII.

ROOKLYN then consisted of several hamlets ; one around the ferry of about fifty houses. A steep hill arose to the west of it, studded with forest trees. On the top were orchards and market farms. The hill extended all along the water front, where each farmer kept his boat to carry his produce over to the Fly Market.

One afternoon, the miller gave Janse a half-holiday, and he started on his long cherished plan of a search for some tidings of his father.

On the Heights was a battery of eight guns. This he first investigated. Then down in the hollow, and up another hill, at the present corner of Court and Atlantic Streets, called "Cobble Hill." Here a charge had been made. The grass of summer, and the snows of winter had covered the ground since the fight; but he picked up arrow-heads and buttons of the Forty-second Highlanders. On Fort Greene the skeletons in the blue clothes and leather buttons of the Continental army were still lying.

He walked down the Clove road to the field where he was wounded. Here he found a broken musket with "P. H." marked on its iron lock, close by a figure clad in the striped, home spun, so often seen on the village streets. He knew the man—one of the neighbors at Uncle Seaman's. He unclasped the gun and took it away with him, to send back to the man's family at the first opportunity. It was a nerve-aching afternoon, for a lad to sit under the trees and see the long hillocks of green grass, and know they were mounds covering the simple folk, his neighbors, who were fighting for their children and their homes.

It was uncertain about his father. He might rest in one of those long graves; but as long as he could find nothing above ground to assure him of his death, he hoped on, that some day he would come home. But why he did not send them some word, they could not understand.

The years rolled on. Still Janse watched and waited. His mother's nervous system had broken down under the prolonged strain. She sat in her easy chair at Uncle Seaman's, a confirmed invalid, patient and submissive in her widowhood, for she had given up all hope of ever seeing her husband again. Janse's visits home were the bright days in her calendar. Gretchen was as tall as her mother, straight as an arrow, dark-eyed, and

crimson lipped. She came down one summer
to visit Janse at the miller's. Fortunately, it
was the time of the summer excursions, for
the British army enjoyed every opportunity
for pleasure.

Janse took her in his row-boat, to see
brilliant ladies and British officers in their
boating parties on the East River. Uncle
Seaman's liberality had provided her with
clothes equal to any of the high-born dames ;
but she was only a country-bred little rebel,
while they had never done much greater
work than dance and play on the spinet ;
consequently Janse was somewhat surprised
to see Captain Lushington leave his gay
friends at the Battery, and motion him to
approach with his boat, into which he stepped to greet Gretchen, whom he invited to
attend a race at Flatlands, by the horses of
noblemen and gentlemen. Janse at first hesitated, but the Captain urged his case so

strongly, he consented; for it was of interest to him to appear on good terms with the British. He could disguise his real sentiments better. He frequently had business with the Commandant, for the Wallabout Mill supplied the British on Long Island with grain. He kept his eyes and ears open, and many important movements he was able in this way to send to General Washington.

The stone house at the ferry was called the "King's Head Tavern," where parties came from New York to eat fish. The host was a strong royalist; and now, in honor of the Queen's birthday, there was to be unusual festivities. Early on the appointed day, Gretchen was at the miller's door in her riding habit. A servant brought her horse up, a dapple gray pony, as the black horse which bore Captain Lushington pranced up, the admiration of the black faces which crowded the kitchen windows watching their departure.

Gretchen was so happy she could have sung with the birds, as they rode along. The dew was still on the leaf and flower that soft June morning, as they rode past the camp at Bedford, where the regiments had dug barracks out of the earth and covered with planks.

When they reached the field, the first thing in order was a hunt. Captain Lushington bowed to every person they met. Gretchen's cheeks were aflame as she noticed the attention she attracted. Noble ladies laughed and chatted in French to him. Some sentences she could understand, for he had taught her some of the language in the long winters he had encamped near Uncle Seaman's. When they had all dismounted he led her to a seat upon the stand to view the horse race. After that the whole party adjourned to the tavern at the ferry, for dinner. Gretchen followed the ladies from the dressing to the

dining-room, where Captain Lushington
awaited her. Lady Alice, his cousin, who
had often heard of the kindness of the Seaman's to her favorite cousin, took especial
pains to make her at home among strange
faces. In the evening the tavern was lighted
with two hundred wax candles. The best
band on Manhattan Island made the British
at home playing their national airs.

The rebels were not allowed to approach
nearer than the Heights, where the country
folk looked in mingled wonder and wrath.
But their time was coming ; right will conquer in the end.

Janse one evening took Gretchen in his
row-boat around the ferry, past the Heights
and the house upon the summit where General Washington and Lafayette, on the night
of the battle on Long Island, decided to
retreat to New York. They counted in the
vicinity eighteen line of battle ships, and sev-

enty-five transports belonging to the British navy. It was enough to awe and paralyze the few people in rebellion to see the strength of the enemy ; but from the half-starved people in the cabins along the coast, from Maine to Georgia, arose the incense of constant, fervent prayer to Him who led his chosen people in their efforts to be free.

Near the mill at Wallabout lay the prison ship " Jersey," the hulk of a British vessel, worn out and anchored there on the beach. In the winter they dug a trench in the snow and threw the dead in. In the summer they brought them from the ship every morning and buried them along shore.

The thousand prisoners on board were sick with all manner of diseases that want and misery could bring upon them. Every one was afraid to go on board. Janse often rowed around the vessel and saw the white faces crowded close to the port-holes for a

breath of air, and always looked for his father.
At last he made up his mind he would risk
disease, and ask permission of the miller to
go on board and sell meal. This the miller
granted, with the understanding that he was
never to go in the clothes he ordinarily wore;
he must keep an old suit in the boat-house
to wear when he went on board.

IX.

THE first morning he went, the miller's wife roasted chickens for him to take on board to the sick. He noticed the fish in the water, darting and sporting. They were free, while the men he was going to see were dying for air.

Many, many mornings he went on board, and almost every time decided it would be the last. The foul air coming out of the hold sickened him. The emaciated men haunted him ; but each time he went àgain to give them a bit of comfort and look for his father.

One morning he went as usual. He clambered up the ladder hanging outside, and saluted the marine walking the deck, gun in hand, and saw him approach the officer of the day for orders. Janse looked around on the pale, haggard men, who were allowed to come on deck in companies, to breathe the fresh air and feel the sun. He noticed one face, the skin drawn tightly over the bones. The sunken eyes looked so eagerly at him it startled him. He did not remember the face, when a wan smile lit up the countenance and he saw a resemblance to Katharine. Could it be his father? Was it possible for five years to change anyone so much? He had always remembered his father as he left home, a tall, broad-shouldered trapper. Could this thin, broken down old man be he?

He looked again, and the smile reassured him, it must be! Fortunately the officer's eyes were down writing the order, or he would have noticed Janse turn extremely pale, and lean up against the railing for support. He could only smile an answering recognition, when he was obliged to leave the vessel. He never knew how he reached home. The reality unnerved him. So many mornings he had gone on board and heard, the cry, " Bring out your dead," and left, thinking his father might be one of them, that it was almost too much joy to think he was alive. But Janse knew he could not live long in that pest-house. The next day, when he visited the prison ship, he dropped a slip of paper at the feet of one of the prisoners he was acquainted with addressed to his father, asking him to be at a certain porthole the first stormy night. How anxiously the next day he watched the clouds. On the second evening, a thunder storm came up. Fast and furious poured the rain on the land and water, while thick darkness settled down.

Happy Janse swam out to the appointed

place, and talked for some time to his father, while the sentry was at the other end of the boat. O the questions and answers! For five years Mr. Van Scoy had not heard from home, until he had heard the prisoners speak of "Janse the miller." The once strong man was crushed and despairing and would fain take heart of the lad, who cheered him with promises to try every means for his release.

The miller gave him a holiday on the next day, to go to New York and try to get his father exchanged. His first thought was of Captain Lushington, whom he found with a party of officers, bowling nine pins on the green opposite head-quarters, the present number one Broadway.

Janse explained his business, which the Captain entered into heartily, but thought Janse had better see the Commandant himself, to whom he would introduce him. When he entered the General's presence, he was faint from nervousness, but the thought of the haggard man, shut down in the foul heat of that prison hold, strengthened him. The General heard his story quietly, then said :

" Have you been on that pestilent ship ?"

" Yes, sir," he answered.

" What was your object in going to almost certain death."

" I took food to make them more comfortable, and I was looking for my father."

"And you found him, and want him exchanged ?"

" Yes, sir," and Janse's large dark eyes were raised imploringly to the General's face, who sat for a few minutes shading his eyes with his hand ; for before them came the stately home of his childhood, and again he was a boy, and the noble, hearty gentleman, his father, was preparing him for his first hunt. He could almost feel the wind again in his face, as he dashed over fence and ditch the first one in at the death, and could hear again his father's shout at his success. But many years he had been sleeping in the parish church-yard, and the General's eyes were dimmed when he turned to Janse and promised to investigate and send him word by Captain Lushington.

Janse had no opportunity of visiting the Jersey before he received the papers of exchange. Captain Lushington offered to drive him up to Uncle Seaman's if he wished to go, and make arrangements about his father's return.

Two years had passed since Janse had been at home. He left Captain Lushington at the tavern, and walked down the lane alone. He stopped at the cabin. The latch string was drawn in, and everything left in order for the family's return. He went on to the Big House, stopping at the slaves' quarters outside to have a chat with Cæsar and the picanninnies. Dinah was in the kitchen of the house, who said all were out riding but Gretchen, who was in the end room spinning.

Janse walked through the rear hall and watched her, stepping lightly backwards and forwards, her fingers stained with the blue dye of the wool she was spinning. Her dress was a white cambric short gown, and green silk skirt, red stockings and high-heeled slippers. Her dark eyes softened, and the color came in her creamy cheeks when she saw Janse.

The good news was soon told, and all was rejoicing when the rest came home; although it was thought best not to inform Mrs. Van Scoy until her husband was really out of bondage. Her illness and her removal to another part of the house making this possible; the knowledge of Janse's visit being kept a secret from her.

8

The next morning Uncle Seaman returned with Janse in a long covered wagon, in which they placed a bed and pillows to make Mr. Van Scoy more comfortable on his journey home. The pass for his release was sent on the Jersey the night Janse reached Brooklyn, but his father could not come on shore until daybreak the next morning.

Soon after midnight Janse was dressed, and thinking it must be nearly morning, went down-stairs to the kitchen, the light from the fire in the great fireplace shone on the face of the tall clock, showing the hands to be at one o'clock. He threw himself down on the " settle," and slept until Uncle Seaman awoke him as the first rays of the sun appeared in the east. They were soon on the beach waiting. How long the time seemed until eight o'clock. They saw the small boat put out from the Jersey, and at last reach shore. Janse lifted his father in his strong arms and carried him, almost a skeleton, to the house where he was bathed and dressed in his own clothes which Gretchen had sent down, and laid upon a feather-bed, to rest before dinner.

The miller's wife had cooked a chicken pot-pie; but Janse could not eat, for a lump which kept coming up in his throat, as he fed his father, who was too weak and ill to feed himself. He was so anxious to get home, that they started, ill as he appeared, early in the afternoon. When they were about a mile from home, they found one of the black boys on horseback, waiting to be assured of Mr. Van Scoy's safe arrival, who dashed off home with the tidings, according to agreement, that Mrs. Van Scoy might be prepared for the meeting. But she, as well as the rest saw that he was too exhausted to be excited, so they received him quietly as though he had been gone but a day, and let him lie on the high bed and drink in his happiness with his eyes. Janse returned to Brooklyn almost as white and ill as his father. All his youth, his mind had been fixed upon the thought of finding his father ; now that it was all true what he had often dreamed of, he hardly knew what to think about now.

But in a week's time he was the happiest lad in Brooklyn ; tall as the miller, for he was nineteen years old, the best runner and jumper in the village, where his bright face and cheery whistle was known in every part.

X.

IME rolled on. The war was drawing to a close. Already negotiations for peace were begun. The colonists hoped it was the last winter they would be obliged to support a rapacious army, whom they hated and feared.

The winter of 1781 was a bitter one. Farmers from the surrounding country brought in loads of wood. Those families who were too poor to buy, were obliged to split up chairs and tables for fire-wood. Many suffered severely. Janse went up Christmas week to see his father, who was able to walk down to the village store, and live over again his five years in the army, as he recounted the adventures to the farmers, who were too old or too young to go into the army. Sitting on barrel heads, they listened with bated breath to the story of Valley Forge.

There Janse found him surrounded by a listening crowd, who in the winter spent much of their time there. He told them of the suffering in town, and arranged to take down a load of wood, which the farmers joined in sending to their friends in distress.

One afternoon in the winter of '81, Janse went down to the mill at Red Hook, for a load of special grain. The East River was frozen over. The soldiers were dragging cannon from Staten Island to New Jersey on the ice. He came back through Red Hook Lane, passed quiet farm houses, the great fires in the kitchens illuminating the windows. Here and there a boy would come out of the snow-covered barn-yard and have a chat with Janse. Every one knew him between the two mills.

He passed the Dutch Church, a square, gloomy building, standing in the middle of the King's highway, the present Fulton Street. Then down to the wagon-yard near the Ferry where all the horses and wagons belonging to the British army in this part of the country were kept. Here he left some of the grain, then on to the fort, at the present corner of Henry and Pierrepont Streets, the largest on the Island then uncompleted, on the work of which two thousand soldiers were employed. But they were soon to leave their fruitless labor, and even General Raisdesel, commandant, who lived in a small house on the shore, was in constant terror of the rebels carrying him off captive.

He kept a constant patrol around his own house, and every night pickets were stationed around the fort and wagon-house; so when

Janse left the fort he received a pass to leave the limits of the town for Wallabout.

He was cold and tired when he reached home, where he found Cæsar with a letter from Uncle Seaman's, telling him that he had concluded to give Janse a start in life. He had therefore bought De Witt's mill in the road above their old home in New York, and would put him in charge. Janse was delighted, and went over early the next morning to see his old home, which had been occupied all through the war by British soldiers, who had now gone to Canada. How his heart sank when he entered the yard. All the out-buildings were destroyed; even the wood work in the house chopped up for fire-wood, and all the windows broken. There was but the shell of a house remaining.

It took all his spare time the following spring to render the house habitable. The kind Dutch neighbors who had remained in town under British protection, helped him; one woman coming in to white-wash, while another scrubbed the floors. The old lilacs nodded in the kitchen window as of old. Janse made the kitchen garden, before he furnished the house with the load of furniture he brought down from the cabin. The few china plates were hung for ornaments upon the white-washed walls, the brass candle-stick and snuffers shone brightly on the shelf. The mahogany chest stood in the familiar corner. The claw-feet chairs pressed the clean sanded floor, and Janse thought it looked as natural as it did six years before, as he took a last look before locking the door, and jumping in the wagon to go down to the ferry.

With a light heart he brought them home, through the present Wall Street, then famous for its splendid shade trees, up to the old door, where all the neighbors were assembled to welcome them home.

They settled down to the old life ; but how changed. Mr. Van Scoy's broken health only enabled him to assist Janse at the mill. Mrs. Van Scoy was a confirmed invalid. Janse was the bread winner, and Gretchen the housekeeper. The mill prospered while the British remained, but at last the time came for them to bid farewell to our shores.

November 25th, 1783, was the day fixed for their departure, and the entry of the American Army. The British marched from all parts of the town to Whitehall in the morning. They refused to leave until noon.

Janse went down to the Barracks to bid his friends good-bye, for they had been kind to him ; then hastened home to prepare for the afternoon. As he passed a house he saw the American flag run up. Immediately an Englishman commanded it to be torn down. This the man of the house refused to do, and his wife appearing upon the scene with a broomstick, beat the foe upon the head until the powder flew out of his wig in all directions, and he was glad to retreat, leaving the flag flying.

Clear and bright shone the autumnal sun through the trees dressed in holiday attire, upon the American procession, marching down the Bowery, General Knox commanding. After the army came all the trades, represented by men at work upon trucks.

Janse stood by a miniature mill. Then came the furriers and Indians dressed in the scarlet blankets, and feathers and beads they so much admired. It was the finest procession ever seen in this country at that time. After all came the whole population of the town.

By three o'clock the last British soldier had left the Island, and General Knox entered

Fort George at the Battery. The British flag waved proudly over them in derision; for the flag-staff had been greased to prevent any one ascending. Cheers rent the air as they saw the British vessels sailing out in the Bay, and hisses as they saw that flag beyond their reach. But quick as the carpenters in the procession could prepare cleets Janse handed them to Van Arsdale, who began nailing them from the bottom of the flag-staff which he ascended step by step, nailing each cleat before him until he reached the top, when he tore down the sign of the oppressors and flung in on the water, and shook out from its summit the American flag, amidst the booming of cannon, and the shouts of thousands beneath him, victory at last.

XI.

HE city, after the British left it, was desolate indeed. The American families which had fled upon its occupation by the British, now returned to find buildings defaced, gardens destroyed, old friends estranged by the bitterness of party strife, for there were many families who had become royalists because it was to their interest to do so.

Janse's trade at the mill had been almost entirely with the army. After their departure, the mill arms were frequently quiet for days.

Captain Lushington did not leave with the army. He sold out his commission, and bought land at Jamaica where there were many royalists. He built a fine house of the style of his English home, and there, one day he brought Gretchen, a bride.

It was a very hard year for Janse. The mill brought in so little money, he was at his wit's end to provide food for the family. He cultivated his garden; not only raised the vegetables they lived upon, but sold enough to furnish actual necessities. He made up his mind at last that he would try some other means of earning a living. Gretchen had proposed taking her father and mother home with her for the summer the next time she came to New York, then it would not be necessary for him to remain longer at home. She came down unexpectedly and took them back with her in her handsome carriage drawn by four horses, and her liveried servants attending her.

Janse locked the house door, and borrowing a boat of a neighbor living on the river, rowed over to Wallabout to the mill where he had learned his trade. The miller was very glad to secure his services, and made arrangements for him to begin the following Monday. Entering his boat again, he rowed a mile down the river to the house of a Quakeress, whom Uncle Seaman's family were intimate with; she was a widow and lived alone. Janse tied his boat to the stake on the shore, and walked up the path to the side door and knocked.

Rebecca Jones answered the knock, and greeting him warmly said, "Will thee walk in, Janse?" and she led the way into the clean white living room. The floor was scrubbed until it shone, the pine table was spotless, the walls were white-washed, the curtains to the windows were as pure as snow, if cleanliness is next to godliness, this Quakeress was very near perfection in this respect.

"This is Naomi Bunker," said she, as a young girl came in from the garden with a pan of currants in her hands she had just picked.

"Perhaps thee remembers her."

"O yes," said Janse, "Gretchen and I had been many days nutting in the woods with her, when we first moved to Uncle Seaman's." And he shook her hand eagerly; she scarcely raised her large gray eyes, as she murmured some words of recognition, and demurely seated herself on the door-step, and began to stem the currants for tea.

Janse had a long conversation with Friend Rebecca, after she said she would receive him into her family while he worked at the mill. She told him of her own chastenings since they had met before, of her loneliness, and the call she had felt to take in, and watch over Naomi. Her parents had recently died, and she had just recovered from a long illness, and had come to Brooklyn, in hopes that the sea air would restore her health. She had enough of this world's goods, but had no one to take care of her, poor maid. Rebecca's soothing, quiet ministry were working a cure.

Janse thought she made a very pleasant picture as she sat in the door-way, in the shadow of the maple tree, dressed in drab with a white handkerchief around her neck, the ends crossed over her breast, the white cap hiding her hair all but a narrow streak in front where it shone like black ribbon. Her long dark eyelashes were seldom raised from her pale soft cheeks, as her little hands picked off the red currants. She was so small and thin, she did not look as old as she was—seventeen years. The longer Janse looked upon her, the deeper grew a feeling of half protection, half pity ; he did not exactly know what it was, only he realized that some

9

influence made Rebecca's house a pleasant home in anticipation, as he very cordially thanked her again for being kind enough to take him to board.

He brought his trunk over that night, and the next day being Sunday, he attended the Dutch Church. In the afternoon, Rebecca and Naomi sat perfectly quiet and read their Bibles. Janse would have liked to have walked around the barn, and looked at the cattle, but he respected their feelings and remained in the house until evening, when he ventured to ask Naomi to walk down the shore with him, when she hesitated, Rebecca said :

" Thee had better go, for thy doctor said thee must have plenty of sea air. Then putting on a close silk bonnet, she walked with Janse down through the orchard. Her silence embarrassed him ; the girls whom he knew in the village, were always ready to talk, but this one was unlike any he had ever seen. Coming to an old boat drawn up on the beach, he asked her if she would rather rest awhile, she did not answer, but bowed and walked slowly along. Presently they turned back to the house without exchanging a dozen words. Janse felt disappointed; he felt angry with the deep bonnet which hid her face from his view. He wanted to see those dark gray eyes he remembered so well. he consoled himself with the reflection, that if he lived any length of time in the house with her, she would learn to be more friendly with him.

The next day Pinxter, (Whitsuntide), he invited her to go with him down to the ferry stairs, and see the slaves dance for the silver pieces the gentlemen gave them; for this was a great holiday with the colored people. Raising her luminous eyes, she said in her soft low voice :

" I am constrained to tell thee, Friend Janse, that I cannot go and see my poor colored brother in bondage, made the sport of idle men."

" Colored brother !" exclaimed Janse, and then the comparison made him laugh outright.

She looked at him calmly, and answered :

" If thee had read thy Bible well, thee would know we are all of one family ; but I mean not to argue with thee, friend Janse, I have only given my testimony."

Janse did not invite her to go out with him again. He gave up trying to make her talk. He could not help noticing how neatly she always looked and how quietly she moved around the house. She rested him every time he came in from the noisy mill.

Sometimes he would catch a first glimpse of her as he came over from the water, sitting on the long grass in the orchard, knitting or

. hemming the white handkerchiefs she always wore around her neck.

Rebecca owned a boat, which he used in going to and returning from his work. He had fastened the boat and stood a moment to enjoy the particularly fine sunset, then turning suddenly, he saw Naomi leaning against an old apple tree, so absorbed in the view that she had not heard him arrive. She was looking with eyes transfixed through the golden sunset to the land, where all her family had gone before. Tears fell unheeded from her eyes ; her entire mind was with the past and future. Creeping softly behind another tree, Janse waited for her to regain her composure and enter the house before him. The scene impressed him strongly, he could not analyze his own feelings. She looked so spiritual, a terrible dread came in his mind that perhaps she was not long for this world ; the thought cut him like a knife.

He followed her into the house, and drank the cup of tea she passed him, and ate the waffles she had baked, but all the while he was picturing a life without her sweet presence in it. It became unendurable, he imagined she had changed in a few days, and was much thinner and paler, really in a decline. He left the house in distress.

The stars were appearing in the sky. Rebecca had gone to the village when Janse came in from the barn. The room was in its usual order, but no Naomi. Passing through he entered the little white-washed shed where the roughest work was done, close by the window which overlooked the river, sat Naomi. She did not turn as Janse came up behind her, and putting his hands on both sides of her head, smoothed down her wet cheeks. She sat very quietly as he gently drew her head back until it rested against him. He asked her what troubled her, and then she told him of her loneliness. He knew his feelings then; it was a longing to take her to his care, and then with the sound of katydids and crickets around them, they learned each other's secret. How she had always thought of her old schoolfellow; but had been too shy at the first to talk much to him of the old times, and then she had thought he could not care for a plain little girl like she. And so the loneliness had grown upon her, the only bright spots in the day being his return to his meals. Now the whole world was filled with the light that never was on land and sea.

When Rebecca returned, she found them sitting together, with the full moon shining on them through the trees. She rejoiced with them. Afterwards talked over ways and means; advised them to defer their marriage for a few years, as they were both so young; but after she had retired to her own room, laughed aloud, as she replaced her Quaker bonnet in its large box. It was just what she had planned, the first day Janse came.

She was very fond of both, and before she slept had taken a mental view of the contents of the chests in the garret, and laid aside an enviable outfit for Naomi, of table linen of her own spinning, and weaving at least ten bed quilts, three down covers, and bed linen without end. And she really thought, as she settled herself for slumber, that she would send to Philadelphia for the drab silk for the wedding dress. She had her own way in the matter ; the two most interested were too happy to think about such minor things as furniture and clothes.

They rowed out on the river in the moonlight. They took early morning walks. They thought the world would hold but one brighter day for them, and that came in October, when the simple service of the

Quakers' made them husband and wife, and then went over to New York to begin housekeeping in Janse's old home, and resume business at the mill.

Mr. and Mrs. Van Scoy remained the rest of their life with Gretchen, only coming down occasionally to see little Naomi and Rebecca, and after many years a little Jansen.

XII.

ALL right, mother; I must hurry, or the boat will be in, and Jansen will not know where to go. He does not know where we have moved," said Ned Smith, as his mother handed him his cap she had been mending, and putting it on his head, he darted off to the ferry to receive Jansen Van Scoy, who was coming over to Brooklyn to visit his friend Ned Smith.

Years had passed since his father, a young man of twenty had viewed the departure of the British from our shores. Now his son Jansen, was coming over to the place once so familiar to him. Ned reached the new ferry in time to greet Jansen.

" I'm glad you came this morning, Jansen, for all us boys are going to see if there are any eggs left in the birds' nests in the woods on Clover Hill, this afternoon."

" Where's Clover Hill ?"

Why, on your left hand, right before your eyes. The teacher said he would give us an hour off from school this afternoon. We are making a collection of all varieties of eggs. Will you go in school this afternoon ?"

" Yes."

" Well, I don't want to be late ; let's race. One, two, three," and off they ran down Furman Street to the main road, up the road until they came to the school. At three o'clock the boys were released, and were soon scattered over Clover Hill, a thick woods, between the ferry and the Navy Yard. In their racing and playing in the woods, Ned Smith's mended cap became a complete wreck. When he reached home bareheaded, his mother said he might go after supper and buy a new one.

Brooklyn, in 1824, was a sleepy country village nestling in the thick foliage of many fine trees. The old country road, the pres-ent Fulton Street, was the highway which ran through the Island, from the ferry to Montauk Point; on each side of this as far as its juncture with the road from the new ferry, the present Main Street, were most of the dwellings in the village. The stores were all on this road within a few blocks from the ferry. To one of these Ned and Jansen went for a cap. While the hatter was trying to fit Ned's head, some one in the road cried, " Fire ! fire !" that was enough for the boys.

They ran to the firemen's house, in the hall of which were always standing large buckets to be used in case of fire in the village. Every house had buckets in the hall, but in the firemen's house were an extra

number. Ned and Jansen each seized one
and ran to the pump at the corner of the present Fulton and Hicks Streets. Then, forming in line with the rest of the people, men,
women and children, they passed the filled
buckets down the line to those nearest the
fire, which proved to be the chimney at the
bakery on the right hand side of the road.
Every one worked with a will, not only out
of kindness to the baker, but in their own
interest. It was the only bakery in town.

Ned Smith had that very afternoon run up
the steps to the bake-shop. It did not
require very great exertion to subdue the
flames ; but the boys stood on the corner of
Buckbee's Alley and discussed the matter,
listening to Mr. Hick's description of his dis-
covery of the fire as he was coming out of
Coe Downing's Stage House.

"Jansen," said Ned, as they put out the
candle before retiring at night, "I'm going

to be the first one at the new market which
is to be opened to-morrow.   Do you want to
go too ?"

" Of course I do ; call me early."

In the chilly dawn, they crept out the back
gate to the old ferry road at the foot of
which stood the new market, close by the
ferry stairs.   Already the business of the
day had begun.   One of the butchers said if
Ned would come down in the afternoon, he
would make it all right with him.   Ned said
he would, but he thought he must devote
most of his time to his guest.

After breakfast, they went into Ludlow's
orchard to see the firing of a target company,
which had come over from New York.   Jansen, in his excitement, stood very near the
target, and received a ball in his side, as they
thought; fainting, he dropped upon the
ground.   All was confusion.   One said, run
for Dr. Wendell—run for water—take him

over to Mr. Birdsall's. When Mr. Hicks appeared upon the scene, he quickly arranged a stretcher out of a door, and had Jansen carried to Dr. Hunt's, the whole village, apparently, following. The genial, kind physician examined Jansen carefully, and found the ball in his clothing; he had escaped unhurt. When he found this out he quickly jumped up as well as ever. But the citizens were aroused to the danger, and holding a meeting in the evening, passed resolutions forbidding target companies shooting in the village.

After Jansen had been talked to by Father Snow, whom he had met upon the road, on the Providence which had spared him, and been sympathized over by Mrs. Smith, he ate his dinner, and went with Ned down to the market to see what was wanted.

The butcher explained that the old flag which he had for so many years run up on the flag-staff at the ferry, had become too worn and thin for further use. He wished the people of the village to contribute enough money to purchase a new one. He had written several notes upon the subject, which he wished Ned to carry to their addresses and return him the answers.

This Ned agreed to do. Taking Jansen with him, they went first to Mrs. Duffield's, opposite the old Dutch Church, then to the Pierrepont Mansion on the Heights overlooking the Bay. Next to the large stone house shaded by willows, on the present Hicks Street, where they again met Mr. Hicks, who insisted upon their coming into the house and having a glass of cordial and a piece of seed cake. Then to Mr. Middach, a pleasant frame house, where they were kindly received by Mrs. Sands, who was known and loved by every child who attended St. Ann's Church. She gave them some fruit, and told them she hoped to see them in church the next day.

The gentleman had said they might deliver as many as they chose that afternoon. Ned thought they would try one more. Friend Seaman, a Quaker, who lived in the village. When they gave him the note, he said :

" I cannot give to an outward symbol, but I will give ten dollars to assist in taking down the old flag."

Going back to the market, they delivered their notes and messages, received pay for their services, and then betook themselves straight to Mrs. Flower's candy store.

Sunday morning they attended St. Ann's Church, but Jansen was so absorbed and dazzled in watching the sunlight on the marvelous chandelier suspended from the ceiling he paid very little attention to the service. That chandelier was the pride and admiration of the whole village.   It was the gift of Mrs. Sands for whom the church was named.

"I say, Jansen," said Ned, "do you see that house on the corner of Dock and Front Streets ?   Well, it's haunted."

"Haunted ! how do you know ?"

"Why all the boys say so ; catch me going past it at night !"

"O come on down," said Jansen, "let's look at it."   As they approached the house they saw a strange looking woman laying cobble stones in the street.

"That's her," said Ned.

"What is she doing that for, is she too poor to hire it done ?"

"No ; she is rich, but she says no one sees her as she turns her back to the middle of the road.

"Sometimes she sits on the housetop all night, to keep cool, she says.   The other day, when mother crossed the ferry, Mrs. Fisher had her pocket full of eels, carrying them home from Fly Market.

"But come on, here is Mr. Patchen. Good morning, sir, any errands for me to do to-day?" said Ned.

"Well, as you are a pretty fair boy, Ned, you may go every afternoon down to the ferry to the 'Travellers' Inn' where the New York papers are left for distribution, and bring mine up to my house."

"Thank you, sir, I'll be there," and the boys stood still in the street and watched the old gentleman pass down the road. He was dressed in buckskin trousers, a dark brown coat, and a broad brimmed hat placed low on the back of his head, and was the best known man in the village.

Every afternoon that summer Jansen and Ned, after school, took a regular tour around the village, generally stopping at Furman's Stage House to see the stage start for

Jamaica and Flushing ; then down to the ferry to listen to the ferryman, as the time approached for the boat to leave the wharf, stand at the head of the ferry stairs, and call out, " Over ! over !" to hasten the passengers down to the wharf.

One day as they were taking the papers up to Mr. Patchen, they met a wagon loaded with silver, followed by a crowd. Curiosity prompted them to join it. It turned up the road until it reached Mr. Patchen's door. It was the money the city wished to pay him for using his land which he refused to surrender. When the person in charge asked Mr. Patchen to come out on the street and accept the money, he sat quietly in his arm-chair smoking the pipe he usually carried in his hat-band. At last, the patience of the men being exhausted they picked him up, arm-chair and all, and sat him on top of the silver, and left him in possession.

" Hurrah, Ned !" said Jansen one morning, "the day at last has come !"

" Oh, take another nap, it's too early yet."

" I can't rest another minute. I've been thinking all night of what my father has told me of General Lafayette, how he left his home and family in France, and came over here when he was only twenty years old, to help our countrymen fight for liberty. How he fitted out vessels with his own money, and freely offered his time, his fortune, and his life, if need be, to our cause.

" Father says he remembers how bright and grand he appeared to him, the night when the Continental army left Long Island after the battle in which father was wounded. His military coat came up high at the throat around which he wore a white handkerchief, epaulets on his shoulders, and bright buttons down the front. And now to think he is in New York, and is really coming over to

Brooklyn to-day, and we shall see him ! I
wonder if it's going to be a pleasant day,"
and Jansen sprang to the window to catch
the first rays of the sun lightening the eastern
sky.

" It's going to be a glorious day, only very
warm. I'm going for my breakfast.

The boys were at the ferry a long time
before they saw the crowd, which always
surrounded General Lafayette while upon his
visit to America, embark from the New York
side of the river. They watched the boat's
progress through the water, then, amid the
music of the band and shouts of the people,
this grand old hero stepped upon Long
Island once more, under circumstances as
unlike as possible to those in which he had
left it.

The procession formed; military and fire
companies, Hibernian and Masonic societies,
all the carriages in the village, and citizens

on foot, to the ground where the Apprentices' Library was to be built.

Addresses were made, the children sang, and General Lafayette laid the corner-stone of the new building.

Jansen and Ned had an uninterrupted view of the whole proceeding from their elevated position on the high branch of a tree.

After the exercises were over and the procession disbanded, Jansen and Ned followed the carriage which contained General Lafayette to the inn, where dinner was served to the invited guests. As they were well known they were allowed in the kitchen where they could hear at periods the General's voice.

Late in the afternoon one of the black waiters said to them: " I heard the General's carriage ordered up to the door. I think he is going to make a call on the Heights."

Jansen and Ned ran out of the door and

up the steps at the foot of the hill which led
up to the Heights. They crossed the corn
fields and kept in view the carriage coming
up the highway. It turned down the road
leading to the Pierrepont mansion, General
Lafayette looking eagerly out and talking
earnestly to Colonel Fish of the memorable
night when General Washington and he in
that very mansion arranged the flight of the
American army from Long Island by signals
displayed from the flag-staff upon the roof of
the house.

His old commander and friend had gone
to his reward. He could hardly have antici-
pated the wonderful progress this country had
made in twenty years, but General Lafayette
rejoiced to see the people, whose cause had
been so near his own heart, more than
successful.

At the mansion gate the boys were obliged
to leave him, after giving three cheers with

those who had followed the carriage. Where-
ever he went the same love and enthusiasm
awaited and followed him. Next to Washington the American nation cherished the
memory of Lafayette and his kindness to
them.

The boys then went to Duflon's Garden,
where they had apples and milk, and then
slowly walked back to Mrs. Smith's for Jansen's bundle which he wished to take home
with him.

Ned bade him farewell at the ferry stairs;
each vowing to be true boys and true men,
loyal to the country whose struggles had
been so clearly revealed to them on that day.